Tree

AF350056

Ben Goren

ISBN 978-93-5458-806-8
© Ben Goren 2021
Published in India 2021 by Pencil

A brand of
One Point Six Technologies Pvt. Ltd.
123, Building J2, Shram Seva Premises,
Wadala Truck Terminal, Wadala (E)
Mumbai 400037, Maharashtra, INDIA
E connect@thepencilapp.com
W www.thepencilapp.com

All rights reserved worldwide

No part of this publication may be reproduced, stored in or introduced into a retrieval system, or transmitted, in any form, or by any means (electronic, mechanical, photocopying, recording or otherwise), without the prior written permission of the Publisher. Any person who commits an unauthorized act in relation to this publication can be liable to criminal prosecution and civil claims for damages.

DISCLAIMER: *This is a work of fiction. Names, characters, places, events and incidents are the products of the author's imagination. The opinions expressed in this book do not seek to reflect the views of the Publisher.*

Author biography

Ben Goren is a writer who spends a large amount of time thinking about things. Sometimes there are too many thoughts and they start to form into a shape of their own and threaten to take over. When this happens he feels it's better to release them into The Discourse to make some room for new, less aggressive, thoughts.

CONTENTS

Tradition

Once upon a time there was an enormous Field. And in that Field was an astonishingly huge tree, its trunk as wide as a house. The Tree stood in a very large Meadow. Every year the Tree produced a smörgåsbord harvest of fruits, nuts, and leaves. It provided the only shade in the Meadow, and it fed the animals who lived there.

A stream running through the Field led into a small pond, where the largely aquatic inhabitants lived off what could be scavenged and what flowed down to them from the Meadow. Life in the Field, and especially the Meadow, centred around the Tree, and its presence divided all the residents into broadly two types of animal; those in the tree and those on the ground. Lets call them TreeKind and MeadowKind. Of the TreeKind, the Snakes and the Monkeys called the shots.

The Snakes had a nest right at the top of the main trunk, and the Monkeys lived amongst the branches. The two had at first come to form an informal agreement. If the Monkeys didn't eat too much from the Tree, the Snakes would refrain from biting them. The Snakes were born in the Tree and knew nothing but the Tree. A passing bird once asked why they were in the Tree.

"It's where we've always been", came the reply.

"We are in the Tree because the Tree needs us. And because we know the Tree better than anyone else that gives us the right to protect the Tree. It kind of belongs to us really".

In the Spring the Snakes ate the freshest fruit and leaves and in the Autumn they would have first pick of the ripest nuts to store away for Winter. The Monkeys were born on the ground but would live in the Tree as soon as they were old enough to climb it. They appreciated life in the Tree. Sometimes a Snake would bite a Monkey, who'd then fall out of the Tree, never to be seen again, but the Monkeys regretfully accepted this as a part of life. The Monkeys could have left the Tree and lived on the ground, but what kind of life would that be?

Truce

So a kind of Truce came to pass. The Snakes allowed the Monkeys to eat a substantial but specific amount of the Harvest per season. In return, the Monkeys would manage the Fall Down, the process of selecting and delivering the fruit, nuts, and leaves to be given to the animals who lived outside the Tree.

Each season's harvest from the Tree was calculated, categorised, and allocated by the Snakes. The Snakes ensured the Monkeys were always allocated more than they needed and in return the Monkeys carried out their side of the Truce faithfully. The Monkeys reported Tree news to the MeadowKind, and occasionally handed out extra harvest to a selected few "on behalf of the Tree". The Snakes were rarely seen and even more rarely heard.

Most of the other animals in the Field spent a lot of their time in the Meadow at the base of the Tree, collecting the harvest which Fell Down, and enjoying the comfort of the shade. All the animals agreed the Meadow was a good place to live and that it was important to protect the Tree. They paid close attention to the Fall Down because for most of them, they and their families directly depended on it.

They didn't often notice the Bees pollenating the flowers on the Tree, or the Goat who ate the roughage so that the flowers could grow in the Meadow. No-one watched the Beaver make the damn to collect the water they drank in the pond.

Petition

In a normal year, there was always just about enough fruit, nuts, and leaves to ensure that very few animals in the Field ever went hungry.

A succession of bad weather stretching over several years had however caused the Meadow to wilt and the Tree's succeeding harvests to become obviously less abundant. To make matters worse much of the harvest that did Fall Down was of an increasingly poor quality. It had become a cause of great concern for the MeadowKind.

So one day some MeadowKind went to the base of the Tree and asked a Monkey what they were going to do about the smaller, poorer Fall Down and the wilting Meadow. The Monkey scurried up the Tree and a moment later a hissing noise could be heard high above them. There was a silent pause. Then the Monkey returned.

"It's not a magic Tree, it can't harvest anymore than it naturally does", came the response.

The MeadowKind persisted, demanding to be told exactly how much harvest was projected to fall. Again the Monkey ascended the Tree to convey the questions. Another loud, sustained hiss slightly shook the Tree. Another pause. The same, but now clearly more rattled, Monkey returned to relay the answer;

"These things are not the responsibility of the Tree. How can you blame the Tree for giving you harvest and shade and a good life in the Meadow?"

Threat

So the MeadowKind went away and thought about what the Monkey had said, and they came up with an idea. They returned to the Tree with the Bears and they relayed a new message to the Snakes.

"Either give us more, and better quality, Fall Down or the Bears will shake the tree until they fall down, naturally."

This time the hissing erupted with sufficient force to cause lots of Monkeys to howl in fear, and with a great rustling of leaves a number of them angrily descended to the lower branches.

"Why do YOU deserve more fruit?", the Monkeys screamed at Bear and his MeadowKind friends.

"What do you know about how to manage the Fall Down?"

"How would you allocate it?"

"If you shake the Tree, it will certainly die in the next storm and then everyone will die. Did you think about THAT?"

"What about the Snakes?

"Do you want them falling on top of you?"

"Don't you know how deadly their bite is?"

"Go away now before they see you!"

"It's for your own good."

Sowing

Again, the MeadowKind went away and thought about what the Monkeys had said, and they discussed at great length what to do. Most of them couldn't climb the tree and shaking the tree just made the Monkeys angry. There was no point demanding more harvest to Fall Down from the Monkeys because the Monkeys controlled the supply on behalf of the Snakes, not on behalf of the Meadow.

Then a Mole had an idea.

"What if ", it said, "we worked together for a few years to gather and save the ripest harvest from the Fall Down and plant them around the Field to create more Trees? Trees that don't hiss or howl at us".

"I live underground", it continued, "I see how far the Tree's branches go. They're not just looking for water in the Meadow, they're looking for an Orchard. Why not turn half the Meadow into an Orchard? Enough Fall Down, shade, and food for everyone!"

This idea excited the MeadowKind but immediately there were concerns about how much harvest would be put to this use and how much would be left for the MeadowKind. There was after all only a limited amount of Harvest the Tree could produce in any one season. The

Squirrels however, had some news that changed this equation. They had been keeping count of the size of the Harvest and the Fall Down and how much Harvest the Monkeys and Snakes were actually using themselves.

It now it was confirmed that the Monkeys and the Snakes yearly needed only half of the harvest which they were currently allocating for themselves. So, if the Monkeys continued using their half of the harvest and donated the other half, the Plan could work. But why would the Monkeys simply agree to this?

"They're all originally MeadowKind", a Deer said.

"We'll ask them to show support for the whole Meadow as fellow MeadowKind".

And, despite the incredulity of some of the other animals at the transparent naivety of this idea, it was rapidly agreed upon. So the MeadowKind went back to the Tree and they told the Monkey to tell the Snakes that they planned to plant an Orchard. There was a brief silence then a response from the Snakes that sounded faintly mocking. A Monkey relayed the politer parts of the Snakes feedback.

"It takes a long long time to grow a tree".

"Can you wait that long?"

"If you don't eat a lot of ripest Fall Down what will you survive on?"

"How do you know your other 'Trees' will make harvest?"

"Won't they use up water for the PondKind, and isn't that cruel?"

"Isn't it best just to trust in The Tree? After all, aren't we all technically MeadowKind?"

The MeadowKind had anticipated that the Snakes would dismiss their Plan. Ignoring the Snakes' bad faith expressions of legitimate concerns, they next addressed the Monkeys directly.

A Fox stood up to speak.

"The Plan works well and can be achieved in ten years if ...", pausing to look around nervously before continuing, "... as a charitable exchange between us, between MeadowKind, you donate to those outside the Tree half of your allocated harvest. Eventually all of us in the Tree and on the ground will have no need for an allocation, and can take our pick from the entire Orchard".

Then one of the MeadowKind got a little carried away and shouted, "You too can live in Trees that don't hiss!".

Power

A ferocious and sustained whistling erupted from the trunk of the Tree, reverberating across the Meadow and the Field. The Monkeys screamed in pain, and darted around the branches to escape the noise, many clapping leaves to their ears. Some fell out of the Tree and couldn't get back in again. Others threw rotten fruit out of the tree in the hope it would disperse the crowd of MeadowKind gathered below.

Then everyone heard the Snakes speak to the Monkeys.

"If you give away half of your allocation, we will reduce your allocation by half ".

The entire Meadow fell silent. This was unprecedented.

The Terms of The Truce, which none of the Monkeys actually remembered was agreed by whom, when, or why, had been invoked. Worse, the Snakes had reminded the Monkeys that the Truce was built on the Monkeys having calculated access to, not ownership of, the Harvest. The Monkeys didn't get to do the calculations and this realisation left them aghast, incredulous, livid, petrified, and embarrassed. Some were all at the same time.

Betrayal

Such had become the comfortable, unquestioned routine of The Truce and the Fall Down year after year, most Monkeys had adopted two assumptions: firstly that the MeadowKind had as much to eat as they did, and secondly that their allocation was constant and protected.

The second of these assumptions had just been blown out of the water leaving a lot of Monkeys wondering whether they were also wrong about the first. The idea that they might be scared them.

They considered their choices.

There were no other trees in the Meadow, and rumours swirled about how unsafe it was on the ground. On the other hand 'Trees that don't hiss' was a compelling selling point for a reason none of the Monkeys felt entirely safe openly talking about. For the Monkeys, everything about the Plan sounded great on paper. More (hiss-less) trees meant more branches and more space for Monkey families and more fruit and nuts and leaves and, well, it was a win-win proposition.

The main problem was that it would all be for something in return in ten years time. Maybe. There were no guarantees the Plan would work but there was a very real possibility it could break The Truce. Were they expected to sacrifice three quarters of their allocation for ten years? What if the Snakes kept allocating them less and less harvest? Wouldn't they starve? How would infant Monkeys survive in such conditions, and what if there's no Truce anymore? If Monkeys are starving how could they run the Fall Down properly, and why should they?

The MeadowKind waited for the Monkeys' decision and listened to their discussions in the lower branches. A late-coming proposition from one of the older Monkeys spiritedly endorsing their Plan, even if it meant terminating The Truce, gave many MeadowKind a feeling that The Argument Had Been Won and they greeted the result with excited anticipation.

Then the decision came.

The Monkeys had caved.

"We've really agonised over this", they told the MeadowKind, "and it's just not realistic. We all as MeadowKind want the same thing, a good harvest, and if the very interesting Plan was possible it might benefit everyone, but in truth it would cost us more than we can survive"

"Besides", it continued, "We barely use the ground and we use none of the MeadowKind allocation. We're the ones who have to live in the Tree with the Snakes and work hard so you get your Fall Down."

Didn't we earn our Fall Down too? I'm sorry, we respect why you think you need a Plan but we're simply unable to help"

Questions

Now the MeadowKind were confounded. They didn't really have anything to offer the Monkeys aside from their Plan, which had basically relied on the possibility that the Monkeys would share some of their harvest allocation, out of a presumed solidarity sense of solidarity. That presumption had now just very publicly evaporated.

A slight touch of panic infused the MeadowKind's discussions. Would mulching rotten fruit onto to the exposed roots help heal the Tree? What if the shade of the Tree was declared a Monkey Safe Zone? Or should the whole Tree just be shaken until all the Snakes fall out? Who would collect the harvest then? Who would own it? Would only the Monkeys pick them? Who would run the allocation? Would the Monkeys become the new Snakes? Was any of this even possible?

Many of the MeadowKind had forgotten about the Plan, given up on it, or were arguing that they were "always done right by the Fall Down, never had a problem, don't know what the fuss is, causing trouble for no reason, helps no-one that, and upsets all the kinds of animals you don't want to"

Tragedy

Mounting confusion about why the Plan had failed, and disagreement amongst the MeadowKind about what to do next, quickly turned into frustration. Rumours swirled, accusations were levelled at The Ones Who Always Speak To The Monkeys, and the MeadowKind began splitting off into loose coalitions broadly formed around different answers to the question of The Main Problem And How To Solve It. Some of these collections advocated more direct solutions than the others.

As time went on and with the Monkeys back at work, it began to seem that Nothing Had Or Would Change so most MeadowKind had turned their thoughts to the upcoming Fall Down, and whether there would be repercussions for having had confronted the Snakes so directly. It was then that they suffered their first casualties.

A group of agitated Fireflies had been campaigning to volunteer their combined light in a direct action to 'Show Their Faces', that would shame the Monkeys into sharing after which The Plan would definitively begin. Impatient with the confusion they went ahead and put their plan into action. Some of the Monkey's faces were definitively revealed for a moment, so the Fireflies succeeded on those terms, but in the faces that were briefly illuminated the MeadowKind didn't see any shame.

What they did see were Monkeys swatting at the Fireflies, a few guiltily eating them, or hiding from them altogether. Sadly, the effort to light up the huge Tree and the danger this put them in took a terrible physical toll on the Fireflies, and after a short while their spectacular campaign terminated. Some of the Monkeys cried on hearing this sad news, but it was not long before MeadowKind heard it said that many Monkeys were accusing them of ruthlessly exploiting the Fireflies.

The only comment to come from the Snakes was: "Morbidly pretty".

The MeadowKind were devastated at the loss of the Fireflies and deflated by the indifference and shamelessness of the Monkeys. The Snakes were at least predictable.

There was an atmosphere of brutal depression. The Plan had failed. Period. There were more pressing concerns anyway. The weather had cooled, food was low, and there was no mood amongst the MeadowKind for tolerating disruption of the forthcoming Fall Down.

Test

The Season's Fall Down arrived and the MeadowKind gathered under the shade of the Tree, awaiting news from the Monkeys on the harvest to fall. The Squirrels had reported another below average Harvest but the Monkeys were busy and upbeat, extolling how important the Fall Down was, and exhorting everyone to Wait Their Turn. Do It For The Tree. Do It For The Meadow.

Soon thereafter, the Monkeys came to hear about the Squirrel's report and issued a statement explaining that "'below-average' was a short term measurement and there were more buds this year than last year which everyone knows means more than average rather than less. Most of the MeadowKind accepted this explanation and didn't really consider what the implications would be if the Squirrels were right. A vocal minority pointed out the Monkeys had not lied like this before, but were largely ignored.

Then, about half way through the first day of the Fall Down, everything stopped. There was some brief rapid hissing, and no more harvest fell thereafter. The MeadowKind looked up and saw fruits and nuts and leaves waiting to be picked, but no Monkeys. A week of no Monkeys and no Fall Down passed. Stories flew around that the Monkeys had been eaten by the Snakes, or that the Monkeys were refusing the work the Fall Down. The next day, a Monkey slowly descended to the lowest branch, and sombrely addressed the crowd.

"The Snakes have become aware that a number of MeadowKind have been taking ripe harvest, CHARITABLY handed to them in the Fall Down, 'out of shade' to plant elsewhere as part of their 'Plan' to grow competing Trees, which as we ALL KNOW will only hurt our Tree"

A tiny voice shouted out "Why will it hurt the tree?", but the Monkey ignored it and continued.

"This will also upset the balance of the Meadow and eventually the entire Field", it intoned.

"How do you actually KNOW that?!" yelled the same tiny voice, but it was quickly drowned out by the hushing and tutting of the voices around it.

"Furthermore", the Monkey went on, "there has been a sharing of harvest, which contravenes the balance of the Allocation, and upsets the normal cycle of the Meadow. As a preventative measure to ensure the health of the Tree, the Meadow, and all the MeadowKind themselves, we have implemented a new BUT FAIR test to determine the Allocation for each MeadowKind."

The Monkey paused briefly to let this news permeate through the crowd.

"Any actions to undermine either the functioning of the Test and the health of the Tree and Meadow will be grounds for a cut in the amount of Fall Down allocated", it declared sternly. "We regret taking this hard but unavoidable step. We ask all MeadowKind for their understanding as we deliver the Fall Down in a way that works FOR ALL OF US", trailing off with a mumbled, "given the conditions".

A heavy angry voice broke a stunned silence. "How much harvest are the Monkeys losing?"

The Monkey paused again, then rolled its eyes. "Our Allocation has always been agreed and it has neither gone up nor down. We all heard the Snakes. We do not own the Harvest, we only process it, and we make none of the rules about Allocation".

"Now," it added brusquely, "Please form your lines for your Allocation Test. We're about to begin"

A buzz spread through the crowd, mostly relaying the parts of the Monkey's message which were most appealing to think about, which was mainly "We're about to begin".

And so, before another question could be asked, hungry MeadowKind began lining up for their Test. The Test comprised one question: How much harvest did you use in the last Season? Each MeadowKind answered the question in good faith, and was duly Allocated two thirds of their answer, to last them until the next Harvest.

Revolt

It wasn't long before the MeadowKind noticed the pattern.

"Why are we only getting two thirds of what we need?", they asked any passing Monkeys, but got no reply.

The MeadowKind felt trapped. If they accepted this Test and it was used every year then they'd slowly starve, by calculation. It was a terrible situation that many blamed on demanding more harvest in the first place.

An Owl flew down too join the conversation. After a while, it was asked for its ideas for how resist this change to the Fall Down. The Owl wasn't sure what should be done but did have an idea for what might be done. Its search for a nest had led it to find a huge hollow in the Tree where it appeared most of the Snakes lived. This Hollow was the perfect home for the Snakes, sheltered from the elements by big broad leaves but open enough to get warmth and rainwater. And in this Hollow they stored the freshest of the Harvest so that they could eat all year round.

The Owl explained that the Snakes on the branches guarding the Hollow were thiner, faster, and more deadly than those in the Hollow which, although large and powerful, rarely left their shelter, or even moved at all.

"It appears the Allocation is run from the Hollow, for the Hollow. Without the Snakes there is no Allocation and no Test", said the Owl, then flew away.

A small group of MeadowKind mulled over this new information and what to do with it. Scaling the tree en masse seemed impossible, and extremely dangerous. So they tried thinking not about how to solve the problem but instead what the actual problem was. And this raised a new question. What would be the solution to a Snake And a Monkey? And then it came to them, and they rushed off for another hurried meeting.

That night, as the other MeadowKind slept scores of Koalas slowly ascended the tree and began occupying the branches, ever higher towards the Hollow. The Koalas weren't particularly fast or strong but they had two things really going for them: gripping trees and gripping objects in their paws.

To the horror of the Snakes in the Hollow, the Koalas were simply picking the 'guard' Snakes off the branches and throwing them to the ground. The Monkeys, seeing the Koalas get close to their favoured areas of the Tree rushed to assist the Snakes in preventing the Koalas getting any further. And whilst both were thusly occupied a group of Squirrels darted through the lower branches of the Tree, now free of Snakes, knocking harvest onto the ground.

In the morning the MeadowKind awoke to a Tree full of Koalas and a feast fit for a proper Fall Down.

Impasse

None of the MeadowKind felt they had been victorious because no-one was sure what the goal of the action had been, although everyone obviously welcomed the temporary relief. And whilst the Koalas occupied the lower branches, the Snakes and the Monkeys still controlled the middle and upper parts of the Tree. The MeadowKind had only won temporary control of one third of the Harvest and had already distributed most of it. The Monkeys and the Snakes still had more than enough to feed themselves. And now the Monkeys were refusing to come down to continue the Tests and the Allocation because they said the Koalas scared them.

This soon became a problem for the MeadowKind because of the erratic way the Squirrels dropped the harvest and because they had no organised way of making sure everyone got what they needed. In the rush to collect the Fall Down Harvest got hoarded and wasted and it wasn't long before the part of the Fall Down the MeadowKind now had control over began to run out. Seeing the food supply wane, a group of very upset Elk moved that butting the Tree would Solve The Problem.

Sadly, the rash and unilateral implementation of this motion resulted in reaping more Koalas from the Tree than harvest. Word got around and alarmed Koalas started retreating down the trunk, with the Monkeys, and then the Snakes, slowly repopulating the newly vacant branches in their absence.

The revolt had failed.

The MeadowKind were despondent. There was no way to beat the Monkeys or the Snakes, no way to appeal to them, and no way to get past them. Many resigned themselves to the thought that the TreeKind deserved their place in the Tree. They wouldn't be called TreeKind otherwise would they, they reasoned. The Fall Down ended, and there were no more Allocations or Tests. The nights drew in, the weather got progressively colder, and both MeadowKind and TreeKind prepared themselves for the harshest season and all quietly hoped they'd be around to see the Spring come again.

Leverage

After a long, bitter, gruelling, hungry Winter the MeadowKind waited for news of the Seeding Count to foretell of the Summer and Autumn Harvests. As they waited for a Monkey to appear with the news, a Rat got talking with a Bee.

"Been a busy year?", the Rat asked.

"Always busy, like they say!", the Bee replied cheerily but then added "We've tried our best", less cheerily.

"Another bad one?", Rat wondered.

"Well, we can only pollenate the flowers that are there, and harvest can only come from what we pollenate", Bee explained.

"So the Allocation, Harvest, Seed Count, it really all does depend on you guys!", and then laughing added,"I mean, imagine if you refused to pollenate the Tree! It's your Harvest really"

"That's exactly right!", pealed the Bee, sadly ecstatic that Someone Had Finally Gotten It.

A thoughtful silence fell between them. Then Rat looked at Bee, and Bee looked at Rat. And they both looked up at the Tree.

Negotiation

A week later, a meeting was hastily convened at the Hollow.

"So what they're saying is ... is ...", stammered the panicked Monkey to the Snakes.

"SSHHHHHPPPPITTT IT OUUUUTT", the Snakes demanded impatiently.

"They're not going to pollenate the Tree unless everyone owns the harvest. They said they'd allocate one third of the total Harvest to share between the Monkeys and the Snakes, and no Spring Buds", the Monkey cried.

"How dare they!", the Snakes hissed angrily.

"They will fail. The Tree's had years of almost no pollination and survived before. It will again. We have enough to get through, and we can eat our own. This will only teach the MeadowKind a lesson in the harsh reality of survival."

The Monkey gulped hard.

"They said if we ignore them they'll ask their friends to eat all the leaves around the Hollow. And they have millions of friends."

For the first time the hissing stopped altogether. This was a real threat. Without the leaves, the Snakes would have much less cover from the wind and rain and many of them would freeze or possibly drown. Low food could be tolerated, but exposure couldn't. The Tree fell unusually silent. Then there was a short hiss, and the scurrying of a few of the more senior Monkeys to the Hollow. After a long while, a Monkey again descended to the lowest branches to address the crowd. Its voice was steady but its eyes spoke of fear and resentment.

"The Snakes say it is against nature and therefore impossibly for anyone but them to own the harvest since they own the Tree. That said, they are wiling to consider an agreement that the MeadowKind can try to grow their own trees and will be a guaranteed half of the Harvest each year, that would be shared with the Monkeys."

The immediate problem with the Snake's plan was that this was the first time most of the younger and not senior Monkeys had heard of it. Hoots of discontent turned into howls of outrage heard sporadically throughout the Tree.

The MeadowKind weren't impressed either.

It felt like they were getting something good, but something had still been taken from them. Why should they share their half with the Monkeys? Why was it that the Snakes ended up with an entire half and wasn't that more even than the surplus they already had?

A Bee flew forward to speak to the Monkey.

"Tell the Snakes, two thirds for the MeadowKind, one third for the TreeKind. That's deal. Take it or huddle for the next storm".

The Monkey scurried away, there was some hissing, the leaves rustled, and a different Monkey returned.

"One third is a ridiculous, unworkable and frankly outrageous demand", it declared.

"Neither the Snakes nor the Monkeys can accept this". A large group of Monkeys enquired why this was being said in their name. Neither messenger nor the Snakes answered.

And so it went on, the Snakes sending a different emissary down each time with another slight concession, and each time the Bee repeated, "Two thirds for the MeadowKind, one third for the TreeKind. That's deal. Take it or huddle for the next storm". The Snakes tried anger, threats, pleas, and bargaining but the answer from the Bees remained the same. They tried offering the Bees a special deal on their honey allocation but the Bees just laughed at them. Spring Bud season rolled into Summer then Autumn. Some Monkeys tried to stop the Squirrels from reporting the predicted Harvest but the news got out anyway: it was the worst yet.

Conflict

On the ground, impatience boiled over into fear then anger. What would the MeadowKind do now? The Bees had to pollenate the Tree. They couldn't survive another year otherwise. Then a Caterpillar crawled to the base of the Tree and called out: "Why do we have to wait for them to give us what belongs to us?", he shouted.

And with that it marched resolutely up the Tree.

Being unable to climb, most of the MeadowKind had dismissed this possibility for themselves, and they watched the Caterpillar's ascent with morbid and fatalistic curiosity. Two Snakes and a Monkey saw the Caterpillar first, and they came at it from three different directions. Slowly, inch by inch, the Caterpillar climbed, never breaking pace, never changing course, heading directly for the Hollow far above it.

The Monkey swung down quietly and hung from a branch just an arms reach from the Caterpillar, one of the Snakes had slithered straight down the trunk towards it, and the other hung from the nearest branch coiling itself ready to strike.

Escalation

In the blink of an eye the Snake leapt out and bit the Caterpillar, which promptly fell from the Tree to the ground, where it lay motionless, dead. The MeadowKind looked away from the depressing scene. They were safe under the Tree but not in it. On the ground, impatience boiled over into fear then anger. What would the MeadowKind do now? The Bees had to pollenate the Tree. They couldn't survive another year otherwise.

More and more of the other Caterpillars however remained preoccupied with the tragedy they had just witnessed, looking from their fallen friend to the Tree, and back again. A quiet fury arose in them. If there was one thing they all knew to be true it was that there were far more Caterpillars than there were Snakes or Monkeys. This unifying realisation was undeniable and they could feel the power of it.

"Why should we wait for them to give us what already belongs to us?", one shouted.

And with that said it resolutely set out up the Tree, followed after a nervous moment of hesitation, by the others. Some of the Monkeys immediately called out pleading for the Caterpillars to return safely home but other younger, stronger Monkeys quickly descended towards the Caterpillars with distinctly hostile intent. As soon as the Caterpillars got to the height of the lowest branches these Monkeys swooped down to pick them off and throw them out of the tree. The speed and enthusiasm the Monkeys put into this task shocked many of the MeadowKind.

Snakes slithered in to bite the Caterpillars and eat them, but they kept coming from every direction, hundreds then thousands of them, too many for the overwhelmed Monkeys and Snakes to completely repel. Noticing this loss of control, the Koalas once again scaled the Trunk, and went straight to blocking the Monkeys and Snakes from attacking the Caterpillars.

With the Koalas warned in advance, the Elks butted the Tree until a few of the Monkeys on the lower branches fell out, scaring the rest of them to the top of the tree. The Hollow was now relatively unguarded and the Caterpillars, despite the best attempts of the Snakes, now proceeded to eat their way through all the leaves covering the Hollow. The Snakes hissed in fear, and impotent rage. They would have to wait for the leaves to grow back next Spring. For the first time ever they faced a Winter possibly hungry but definitely exposed.

Reaping

When Winter arrived the Tree was blown hard in all directions. If all the animals weren't cold they were wet, and if they weren't wet they were cold. And of course they were all very very hungry. The snows came and left. The Daffodils sprouted and achingly, day by day, Spring slowly emerged, until one day the glistening sun was finally strong enough to fill the interior of the Tree with warmth and light. All that had survived the Winter were then astonished to find two things. The first was that the Snakes had all gone, and in their place was now an empty Hollow full of warm rainwater and a few happy Tadpoles swimming about. The second were three young but strong and fast growing shoots of new plants, well spaced apart, in the Field, sprouting not too far from the shade of the Tree.

Allocator

The Spring came and the Bees went to work pollenating the entire tree and the fresh buds the Snakes had previously kept for themselves were declared off limits so that the Tree could harvest to its fullest capacity. And, despite much complaining about 'indispensability' from the Monkeys, the MeadowKind asked the Koalas to take over running the Fall Down. This decision followed a startling incident when an older Monkey, who had taken to dressing in an old Snake skin it had found, suddenly declared that it could talk to the Tree and the Tree had chosen it to be The Allocator.

Order must be restored, The Allocator claimed, for the Tree had demanded it, and, more specifically, that the Monkeys, not Koalas, were the rightful heirs to run the Allocation. It was not long before some of the older Monkeys started to agree.

"MeadowKind weren't adapted for life as TreeKind" and "it made no sense to be excluded from the Harvest when they were the most able to handle it." Some even felt insulted.

Some of the more attentive Caterpillars who had remained in the Tree warned the MeadowKind about The Allocator and the Monkeys growing discontent. The MeadowKind then sent some Eagles to remind the Monkeys that they would happily switch to a meatier diet if they were to see anything that walked or talked like a Snake again. This seemed to tip the balance of opinion. There was a brief commotion in the leaves, then some very loud howls which descended to the ground and quickly receded into the distance.

A short while later, a Monkey came down and informed the MeadowKind that The Allocator was no more. It was roughly around that time that the phrase 'Never trust a Monkey' became a common refrain amongst the MeadowKind. The Koalas were slow but they were at least predictable and reliable.

Cooperation

From that day on, the MeadowKind and the TreeKind worked together every year to ensure that there was a good enough Harvest to feed everyone and nurture the Meadow. Over a few years the sprouts in the Meadow became saplings, then Trees, and after ten hiss-less years there grew the beginnings of an Orchard. And as the trees grew so too the Meadow thrived. The Beavers expanded the Pond, and it came to be as important for the MeadowKind as the Meadow and the Orchard.

The revived Meadow and the new Orchard also helped revitalise the Tree and thereafter followed several years of bountiful Harvests. The plan had worked.

Years came and passed.

The Meadow bloomed, the Pond became wide and deep, the Orchard was strong, and the Tree which shadowed it remained hiss-less. There was so much fresh fruit, nuts and leaves the Fall Down ran from spring to autumn. Some of the Monkeys had moved out of the Tree to the newer trees in the Orchard to assist the Koalas with the Fall Down, and over time they gradually resumed running it, under the agreed scrutiny of selected Koalas. It was a time of comfort and plenty. Summer lit the Field in glorious sunshine.

Sometimes a squabble would break out amongst The Monkeys but it was of little concern to most of the MeadowKind what the Monkeys were fighting about. They simply said, 'Never Trust A Monkey', and with a knowing laugh continued on their way.

Then one day, a new face appeared in the reeds on the bank of the Pond. The baby Monkeys playing there had never seen anything like it.

"Which Tree is yours?" asked the face, its forked tongue flicking in and out of its mouth.

Its two black beaded eyes transfixed the little Monkeys.

"Show me the way and no Monkey will ever squabble with another Monkey again …"

www.ingramcontent.com/pod-product-compliance
Lightning Source LLC
LaVergne TN
LVHW050427160726
843469LV00041B/1258